MARRIETTA MERZ

ADAM CRAIG

Published by Liquorice Fish Books
an imprint of Cinnamon Press,
www.cinnamonpress.com

Print Edition ISBN 978-1-911540-14-4

British Library Cataloguing in Publication Data. A CIP record for this book can be obtained from the British Library.

This story first appeared in the collection, *High City Walk* (Cinnamon Press), in a slightly different form.

Designed by Adam Craig for Liquorice Fish Books.

Liquorice Fish Books is represented by Inpress.

to the memory of my father,
David Craig

*our gold is not ordinary gold,
nor was our mercury ordinary mercury*

MARRIETTA MERZ

ARIETTA MERZ was eventually born on the day the Great War ended. She had been growing fast within her mother when news of her father's disappearance arrived. A pilot, he and his aeroplane disappeared over the Eastern Front just days before the Bolshevik government withdrew Russia from the war. Confused and grief stricken, Marietta's mother vowed not to give birth to the child until her husband returned.

Hope carried Frau Merz and the unborn child through the following months. Yet hope garnered only bizarre rumour. Some claimed Leutnant Merz had been plucked from his cockpit by a midnight eagle, to vanish in a single beat of ebony wings. The writer of one well-thumbed post card assured Frau Merz he had witnessed her husband and his biplane being caught up in the wake of a passing cloud armada, the coursing white brigantines tugging both into the sunrise and beyond the horizon. Reality, that most malleable of commodities, grew threadbare beneath the welter of conflicting hearsay. Despite this, Frau Merz refused to let Marietta into the world.

Then, Armistice Day came. Something in the silence that fell across Western Europe told Frau Merz that her husband would never return. Dry eyed, she went into labour. At the very instant Herr Erzberger signed the official declaration of peace, Marietta was born on a cross-town tram.

Life was a struggle for most Germans in those difficult, post-War times. Many were forced to wander in search of work. Yet none wandered as far and as often as Frau Merz and young Marietta. By the time she was eleven, the child had seen most of the country; from towns and villages weary from combat and continual hardship, to cities humming with discontent and the countryside between. Marietta and her mother went north into what is now Poland, then turned and travelled into Austria. A bare half-week later, they were packed and on their way again.

There was more to their wanderings

than a simple search for livelihood. It was as if the motion of the tram, the first sensation to greet Marietta at her birth, refused to let them go. Its onward striving filled the girl, its urgency spilling into her mother. At first, they convinced each other that the next move would be the last. A good job, a solid roof were just one journey away. Never, though, did mother and daughter stay anywhere for more than a few months.

Marietta had always to move, move, move. The moment she could walk, the little girl wandered around each place they came to. Even at that age, a quiet-voiced part of her soul told her she was searching for something.

Marietta was on a quest. But for what, she did not begin to understand until she received the notebook.

Even with Winter's fingers trailing

through the fallen leaves, the spa town of Baden-Baden entranced Marietta. Her twelfth birthday was close and the brittle sunshine seemed an early gift from the sky. For once, the rattle-tat of the tram's motion was almost absent. Warmed by the sun's face, Marietta sat on a step and watched the street pass at its own unhurried pace.

She noticed the kindly gentleman even before he sat beside her. He was most neatly dressed, dove-grey suit carefully pressed, pocket handkerchief and hat placed just so. Yet his shirt cuffs were a little frayed and soot besmirched the white tongue of each spat as it peeked from beneath trouser hem.

Politely raising his hat, the gentleman settled himself beside her. After a few minutes of companionable silence, he cleared his throat and told

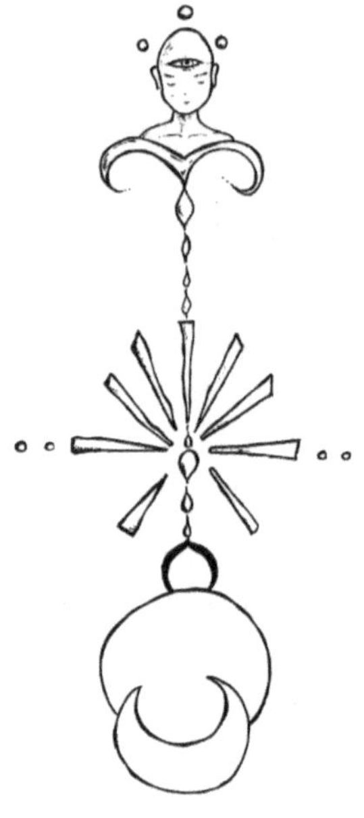

Marietta of a trip he had once made to Persia. Of ruined cities peeking out of the sand and petrified gryphons keeping sentinel over secret bazaars.

'In one,' he said, 'I met a most skilful alchemist.'

Marietta did not know the word. The gentleman with frayed cuffs explained that alchemists transform mundane things into artefacts of pure spirit. This Marietta understood perfectly.

'During the War, my father met a phoenix and was turned into a living flame of purest gold.'

Marietta remembered listening to many such rumours while lying inside her mother. However, this particular story she knew to be true. A little shyly, she looked up at the kindly gentleman.

'It is most interesting that you should say that,' nodded the gentleman seriously. 'I have seen such a bird, you see. It lays its eggs on the banks of tropical rivers. The offspring hatch out as simple sparks; the plumage of living flame begins to come in only after the second moult.'

It was Marietta's turn to nod. She had suspected as much.

After another few minutes of comfortable silence, the gentleman stood, raised his hat again and handed her the notebook.

'Use this wisely,' he told her before strolling away.

Marietta did as she was told. The notebook was always in her pocket, ready to hand. Yet, not until after the year had turned did she place anything inside it. Graz was just coming into bloom when mother and daughter arrived. As Marietta wandered through the Austrian city, she realised there was something here that belonged to the notebook.

Soon, the colours and smells of a special moment in the late afternoon nestled between the heavy covers. For weeks afterwards, she peeked at the remembrance, never opening the book wide in case the sensation should try to escape.

Haltingly at first, she added to the notebook. Guided by the quiet-voiced part of her soul, Marietta grew more confident in recognising those magical seconds when something around her—a place, a shaft of light, a cadenced voice—was verging on pure spirit. Swift and gentle, she decanted the instant from the world and on to a fresh page. Later, whether in the back of a cart plodding towards Wiesbaden or in drab lodgings in Danzig, she had only to open the notebook to be enfolded anew by each transcribed moment.

Gradually, thanks to the kindly gentleman's gift, Marietta came to realise what her quest was for. Ever since birth, she had been unknowingly searching for the secret of transmuting the mundane into the marvellous. The notebook's pages offered the first glimpses of how this might be achieved. Unable to rest until she became an alchemist, Marietta made do for now with being a faithful scribe.

And so the motion of the tram continued to drive mother and daughter in their wanderings. Yet everything has its path and one person's destiny may only travel for a short time alongside someone else's. So it was that, when Marietta was seventeen, her mother left her.

It was October and they were in Lübeck. Frau Merz had found employment at a small shipping company on the quays, cleaning floors and diligently polishing old furniture that held a stronger claim to each office than the people working there.

One grey morning, as she walked to work, Frau Merz paused on the quayside and looked out towards the entrance of the harbour, the sea waiting patiently in the distance beyond. The wind explored her lined face, its damp fingers honed by the Baltic chill. Perhaps realisation came only then, in the pewter light of dawn. Perhaps she had known all along that this moment would come, ever since her husband had vanished.

In any event, Frau Merz raised her raw-knuckled hands as if to take hold of the restless wind.

The next anyone knew, she was gone.

That evening, Marietta quietly left her own place of work. She carried her notebook and a small suitcase, all that she owned inside.

At first, she walked towards the approaching Winter. Wandering through

Estonia and Latvia, she gradually turned eastwards. Never staying anywhere for more than a day or three, Marietta seemed to have no destination in mind, nor any desire to find one. Yet, as her eighteenth year began to enter its Spring, something brought her to Prague.

She stayed for six months. It was the longest time Marietta had been in one place since she her birth.

The city welcomed her, its air tasting of promise and mystery. Within days, she used two of the notebook's precious pages to save the hubbub of conversations in the cafés and the evening light as it caressed the black waters beneath the Charles Bridge. At the end of that first week, she met an artist. Captivated by some inner quality that transcended her careworn exterior, he pursued her with offers of marriage and pleas that she pose for him.

A friend of the painter, equally entranced by Marietta, expended verse after stanza on her beauty.

Marietta was flattered. But all she asked of these men was whether they knew any alchemists. Neither did. Frustrated, she paged slowly through the

notebook. The secret to transmutation seemed just out of reach. There was a way to succeed, she could see, but the path remained hidden. Anxious to find the way, she wanted to move on. Yet something held her in Prague. The rhythm of the tram dimmed and her feet no longer needed to step, step, step.

The pause in her travels lengthened, growing into a sense of expectation.

It came as no surprise when she met the kindly gentleman again. Rain made the crowds hurry, sheltering beneath damp wool and gabardine. Marietta wandered through bobbing umbrella thickets. The pavement reflected each shop window as oil twists light when it reaches for the depths of a pond. A gallery displayed a number of canvases, each bright with impossible landscapes.

'Ah, my dear young lady!' The kindly

gentleman stepped from the shop just as she neared the entrance. The intervening years been unable to touch him. Even the frayed state of his cuffs and smirches on his spats were the same. 'I was just thinking of you.'

Gallantly, he doffed his hat and handed Marietta a small compass on a silver chain. The back of the compass was hinged, the interior decorated with a miniature pelican gripping a ruby-gold feather in its bill. Before she could say anything, the gentleman was gone, lost amid the splashing crowds.

The compass beckoned Marietta closer. 'South by west,' it whispered, pointing the way.

Her new friend led her from Prague. The compass had endless tales to tell of the numinous pathways that lead knowledgeable travellers across the oceans of the world, and of the sights one might find at the end of those hidden roads; from the wings and eyes that are part of the air of Mexico, to the talking masks of Japan.

Together they walked, Marietta and her two companions, the compass and the notebook, the motion of the tram constant and carrying them all three, south by west, a step at a time. Only once did they falter, a dream finding Marietta at the roadside in the midst of a tall stand of trees, the dream tugging at her hands. 'North,' whispered the dream and it whispered in the voice of the young painter she had known in Prague. 'Go north,' the dream urged. Marietta found the motion of the tram less certain and the assurances of the compass did not help her move from the spot where the dream found her. She thought of her mother. She remembered the stories about her father. For the first time, she doubted her path and quest. 'Is this right?' she asked the notebook but the notebook could not answer. Only the dream spoke, although its voice grew less sure of itself. 'Go,' said the dream in the young painter's voice. It did not say where and Marietta waited, wishing the kindly gentleman might find her and point the way.

Another day came to peel away the night and reveal what lay beneath. Doubt sat beside Marietta when she woke. Doubt on one side, the dream on the other. 'Stop here,' doubt told her. 'Go,' advised the dream, the compass whispering the way. 'Go,' advised the dream. Doubt reached for her hand. 'Go,' the dream asked of her, the compass pointing the way. 'Go your way,' the dream said and fell silent. Marietta looked at what the day had revealed. She took up the compass and the notebook, without looking at doubt.

Together, the three companions picked up the motion of the tram. South, by west. Then due south. Always walking until, finally and at last, they reached the Mediterranean. The unblinking sun cast a pure candescence that even the notebook struggled to record. Marietta, the compass and the notebook wove through olive groves and along valleys scented with tamarisk and wild oregano. The motion of the tram held Marietta more strongly than ever. Her faith in the compass and the unspoken destination it sought never wavered, but she did wonder. Wondered whether she would ever find the Alchemist's Path, ever stop searching.

Then, outside a small stone house on

the top of a hill of sun-bleached rocks and knotted trees, she met the small man and his tall wife. The couple stood on a promontory just beyond their little house and, hands offering shade against the sun, watched as Marietta walked slowly up the winding path towards the summit. The woman had skin of purest alabaster which shone like a bright flame in the afternoon, skin that never changed hue no matter how long she stood in sight of the blazing eye overhead. The man, in contrast, was the colour of lovingly maintained leather, tanned by countless days beneath the self-same sky. Only his hair spurned the sun's attentions; that was as startling white as his wife's skin.

'Here,' whispered the compass as Marietta walked the last yard to the summit.

The man's name was Maxim; his

wife's Leonor. They painted, each in their own lean-to at opposite ends of the small stone house. Marietta had seen similar paintings before, in Budapest, Rome, and particularly in Prague. Yet Maxim and Leonor's works were startling, entrancing. They contained everything Marietta's notebook recorded in its pages and more. A missing essence had been distilled into each brushstroke. Marietta recognised it immediately, despite being quite unlike what she thought she had been looking for.

This was true alchemy.

'Here,' repeated the compass.

Marietta believed the compass, but she was reluctant to ask the couple about the alchemy they practiced, or to reveal what she had stored in the notebook. Even so, Maxim and Leonor understood what Marietta wanted. Quietly, without seeming to, they uncovered the secrets of their work. Days passed into weeks, then into months until a year of sunlight and warmth had accumulated around the small stone house, and the rocking motion of the tram dimmed to the point where Marietta hardly knew it was there.

'Here,' agreed the quiet-voiced part of her soul, but Marietta already knew. Her friend the compass had led her well. She stayed a second year, then a third.

Steadily, the notebook filled. At first, Marietta gathered instants as she always had. The sapphire breath of an evening and the clouds flowering above the distant mountains all made their way into the pages. However, as Leonor and Maxim's arts became a part of her skin and bone, Marietta discovered she need not simply record these moments within the kindly gentleman's gift.

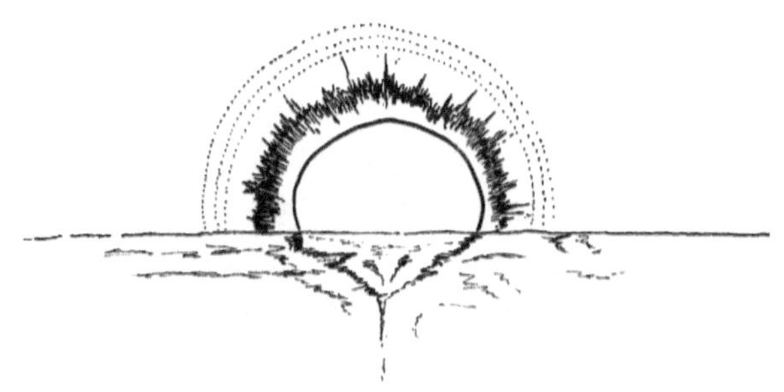

So, a gnarled, ash-grey tree unwound itself into a nest of dancing serpents, each forming the letters of the tree's true name, its inner spirit. On another page, a bird's delicate song built a high tower, whose roots wormed deep into the ground to raise pillars from which the sky was suspended. The creamy paper absorbed the perfume of a late afternoon so that Marietta could transform the scent into glittering constellations, each limning countless moonstone paths, which wound down a hillside transmuted into seas of light beneath an ageless ruby sun.

Each path led to alchemy. Not one path, but many. One for each seeker. Marietta realised this now and saw how her own path threaded from the mundane towards the marvellous. Consequently, one August morning, she silently handed the notebook to Leonor.

Gently, the painter turned the pages, drawing out the essence of each scene, each saved moment in Marietta's journey thus far. Nodding, Leonor handed the book to Maxim, who smiled in recognition.

'Only one page left,' Leonor said.

Marietta knew this was so. The onwards motion of the tram had once again taken hold of her limbs. She waved once as she reached the bottom of the hill. No other goodbyes were necessary and she quietly turned northwards.

The train huffed into Paris, steam adding to the grey unreality gripping the city. It was September now and the taste of impending war was a bitterness that hung on the air. With the devoted compass and almost-full notebook in hand, Marietta left the station. Underneath the chaos of traffic and tramping feet, she could feel a hidden current flowing across the city. Avidly searching each face she passed, certain he would be near, she let the current lead her until the lift began its ascent between the huge steel legs.

'Here,' whispered the compass as they reached the Tower's highest observation deck.

Far below, she spotted his tiny face among the many peering upwards at the steel spire. There was no mistake, no matter the distance. Marietta looked out across the city. The secrets lying beneath the thin skin of concrete and stone were clear now. Each hummed a pure melody that tingled as it entered Marietta's ears. Together, the melodies spoke of inner lives and singular truths. She knew, without the faithful compass needing to speak, that her quest was over. She had found what she had been searching for since birth.

Gripping the notebook in one hand and the compass in the other, she willingly surrendered to gravity's dubious hold and leapt from the Eiffel Tower.

No one, not eyewitness nor newspaper reporter, agreed about what happened next. All talk of crosswinds and hallucinations was quickly obscured, however, by the declaration of war and the terrible events that followed. Only one man remembered the incident, only one man knew what really had happened.

The kindly gentleman in dirty spats and frayed cuffs had watched as Marietta climbed to the top of the Tower and their gaze briefly met before she jumped. With half an eye, he marked where the notebook fluttered to the ground. Afterwards, he retrieved it, unharmed, from the gutter. The brimming leaves fell open to reveal the compass and the final page. The kindly gentleman saw that the notebook had penetrated the world's surface to reveal the truth below. The truth that he had seen and would always remember.

The last page showed Marietta in mid-air. Already, her mundane body was fading as her spirit shook free of gravity's petty grip. Turning with aching grace, her new form headed westward for the luminescent trails criss-crossing the ocean: an incandescent phoenix going in search of new lands, deeper experience and fresh transformations.

'Marietta Merz' was written in a single sitting, without forewarning or forethought — it simply appeared. When it did, there was nothing to suggest it belonged to the same world as *A Locket of Hermes*, which was little more than a few pages of notes and some unrealised ambitions at that point. Several years later, when it was finally time to begin work on *Locket*, The Kindly Gentleman walked into that novel as if he had been a part of it from the very beginning. In their internal chronology, as in their writing, the two stories dovetail and wind themselves into parallel threads that suggest a greater story, somewhere in the background. More hints of that greater story appear in *Child of the Black Sun*, which, as I write this, is an on-going project, begun in the aftermath of the death of my father, David.

My dad was a fan of all my writing but had 'Marietta Merz' as one of his extra favourites. He would often ask me what I was working on and listen closely to my sometimes long, often convoluted, descriptions of works in progress and ideas courted. Sometimes, he claimed what I'd written had gone over his head. It didn't matter, though: he'd like it just the same. At heart, my dad believed in me.

There are lots of other reasons why this special edition of 'Marietta Merz' is dedicated to him and to his memory. Perhaps the most important one is simply that I love him and miss him terribly.

Ti Triskele
Finistère
18th November, 2021

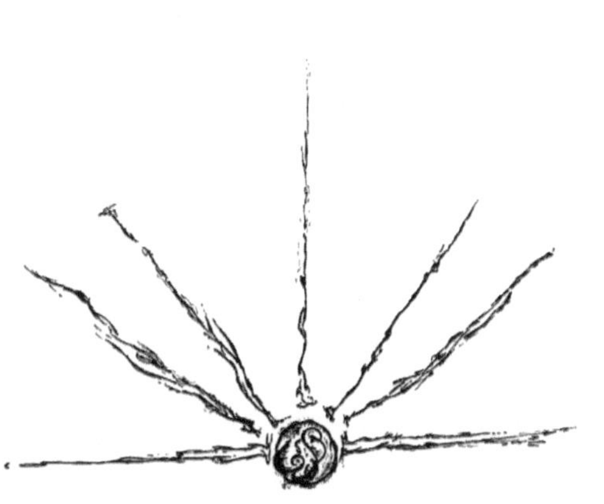

9 781911 540144